ZAC POWER

hardie grant EGMONT

Lunar Strike
published in 2013 by
Hardie Grant Egmont
Ground Floor, Building 1, 658 Church Street
Richmond, Victoria 3121, Australia
www.hardiegrantegmont.com.au

A CiP record for this title is available from the National Library of Australia.

Cover illustration by Craig Phillips
Internal illustrations by Marcelo Baez
Cover design by Simon Swingler

Printed in Australia by Griffin Press, an Accredited ISO AS/NZS 14001:2004 Environmental Management System printer.

1 3 5 7 9 10 8 6 4 2

The paper this book is printed on is certified against the Forest Stewardship Council® Standards. Griffin Press holds FSC chain of custody certification SGS-COC-005088. FSC promotes environmentally responsible, socially beneficial and economically viable management of the world's forests.

LUNAR STRIKE

BY H.I. LARRY

ILLUSTRATIONS BY MARCELO BAEZ

hardie grant EGMONT

Zac Power had his SpyPad earphones jammed in tight, and his eyes closed.

Screaming, loud electric guitar music drowned out all other sounds. Zac was in another world – Axe Grinder's world!

He was tilted back dangerously in his classroom chair, his feet up on the desk. It was lunchtime on Friday – the school week was nearly over. Zac was listening to his favourite band's new single for the 86th time that day!

Sonic Boom was Axe Grinder's latest track. It was so new that it had only been released at midnight the previous day. Zac's older brother Leon had downloaded it at four seconds past midnight. Computer stuff was easy for Leon – he was a spy.

In fact, the whole Power family were spies. Zac liked to think of himself as a SUPER spy. An expert in keeping cool at all times. Always on the lookout for danger. Able to escape the trickiest traps and capture any villain.

The Power family worked for GIB, the

Government Investigation Bureau. Leon took care of everything on the technical side. This left Zac to tackle all the toughest missions.

But GIB was the last thing on Zac's mind. He was concentrating on every note of *Sonic Boom*. Everyone knew that Ricky Blaze, Axe Grinder's guitarist, was the hottest player alive. One day Zac hoped he would be that good, too.

After six months of nagging them, Zac's parents had bought him a totally wicked, ruby-red Gibson Firebird electric guitar. But the new guitar came with a catch – Zac had to attend boring old guitar lessons early *every* Saturday morning. Yawn!

'Zac Power!'

Zac opened his eyes in surprise. His teacher, Mrs Tran, was standing in front of his desk, scowling.

'Take your earphones out *now*,' she said.

This was no way to treat a super spy and future guitar hero! Trouble was, Zac could never say a word about GIB or his missions. No-one at school knew about the action-packed life he led, not even his closest friends. Keeping his identity secret was too important for his spy work.

'Sorry, Mrs Tran,' said Zac.

'Never mind that. The school nurse told me that you missed an important vaccination when you took a day off last month,' said Mrs Tran sternly.

She looked as though she was enjoying herself when she added, 'Off you go to sick bay – she's going to give you the injection immediately.'

OUCH!

Zac headed out of the classroom and walked slowly down the hall. All thoughts of Axe Grinder's incredible new song were swept away by the idea of a big, sharp needle.

He wasn't even halfway to sick bay when a hand reached out of the cleaner's cupboard and grabbed his collar. Zac was yanked in among the brooms and buckets.

The door slammed shut behind him.

A small flashlight lit up the tiny cupboard. When Zac recognised the face of GIB Agent Tripwire, he breathed a sigh of relief.

'Sorry about the scare, Zac,' whispered Agent Tripwire. 'We've got an emergency and had to pull you out of class as fast as possible.'

'So no needle, then?' asked Zac. 'And I get to skip the rest of school?'

'No needle, no school, and keep your voice down,' hissed the GIB man.

Agent Tripwire reached across to a dusty shelf. He lifted up a can of Squeezy Shine floor polish. Zac heard a click.

The whole shelf moved away from the cupboard wall to reveal a hidden doorway. Zac could just make out a steep concrete ramp that led to the school car-park.

Agent Tripwire jumped into the darkness. Zac headed down the ramp after him. A few seconds later Zac heard a gigantic motor roar into life. A powerful headlight came on.

The GIB agent was twisting the throttle on an ABSOLUTELY HUGE motorbike.

'Let's move,' said Agent Tripwire.

He threw Zac a strange-looking helmet and pointed to the seat behind him. In a second they were flying out of the carpark at top speed. Zac was holding on for his life!

Agent Tripwire's voice sounded in the speakers built into Zac's high-tech helmet.

'We have to get you to the Air Force base right away,' said Agent Tripwire. 'The Lightning Strike here is the quickest way to cut through traffic.'

Zac had heard rumours of the Lightning Strike ultra-bike – a top-secret, high-speed vehicle being developed at GIB headquarters. The ultra-bike was painted a rich, dark blue. It packed a motor larger than most helicopters did. Sparkling silver exhaust pipes stretched down the sides.

They were moving so fast Zac could barely suck in enough air to breathe. They passed cars in a blur. Agent Tripwire leaned the massive bike on its side as they tore around corners.

'We've been messaging you on your SpyPad since 7 a.m.' Agent Tripwire was annoyed.

GIB agents were required to carry their SpyPad Turbo Deluxe 3000 with them at all times.

While it looked like an ordinary handheld computer game, the SpyPad was an amazing piece of electronic equipment. A satellite phone, super-computer, X-ray machine, laser, voice scrambler and dozens of other things – all in one small unit.

Zac didn't say anything. He guessed he hadn't heard the messages while he was listening to Axe Grinder's music.

'You've lost a lot of valuable time on this mission,' said Agent Tripwire. 'You did have a full 24 hours but now you've got barely 18 hours and 27 minutes left to get the job done.'

Zac looked over Agent Tripwire's shoulder. The GIB agent was working the touch-screen computer between the Lightning Strike's handlebars. The screen showed dozens of complex words and numbers. Zac noticed their speed – 256 kilometres an hour. This was an awesome ride!

'I'm uploading your mission details to the Stealth Master helmet you're wearing,' said Agent Tripwire. 'You'll like the helmet, Zac. Built in mini-computer, speakers, microphone and camera. Read-outs for air supply and pressure. Special infrared, ultra-violet, heat and night vision.'

Zac's helmet visor blinked on, and his mission began to scroll up the screen.

CLASSIFIED

MISSION INITIATED: 7 A.M.

GIB's WorldEye satellite has photographed BIG's secret new base on the Moon. Intelligence suggests that BIG plans to use the base to sabotage the worldwide webcast of the Rockathon, and steal billions of dollars in donations. BIG's mystery agent, Mirror, broke into the SpaceFortress a few hours ago.

YOUR MISSION:

Proceed immediately to the SpaceFortress and stop Agent Mirror. Prevent theft of donations and sabotage of Rockathon.

*~ **END** ~*

BIG was the sworn enemy of GIB. It was just like BIG to come up with such a plan. Billions in donations to the Rockathon would be a tasty haul for BIG.

The Rockathon was a massive charity event to raise money for countries struck by a tsunami. This freak tidal wave had left thousands of people homeless and starving.

The Rockathon featured the hottest bands from 28 countries. They would perform at a gigantic open-air concert. A few thousand very lucky people would get to watch the show live. The rest of the world could see it on the internet webcast. Coolest of all, Axe Grinder would be the very first band to play!

Suddenly Zac was almost thrown over the side of the Lightning Strike. Agent Tripwire had slammed on the brakes and the ultra-bike went into a slide. It skidded to a halt less than a metre from the loading ramp of a giant Hercules transport plane.

They were on the runway of the Air Force base. Agent Shadow marched down the ramp. 'A quick question for you, Zac,' said Agent Shadow with a worried look on his face. 'Do you know how long astronauts train for their first trip into space?'

'Hmmm,' said Zac. 'I think about three years, at least.'

'That's a shame,' said Agent Shadow. 'I'm giving you three HOURS!'

Keep cool, Zac thought to himself. He had been on some crazy adventures before, but never **SPACE!**

Now aboard the Hercules, Zac took off his Stealth Master helmet and looked around. This was no ordinary transport plane. The inside of the aircraft was like a cross between an enormous gym and a lab.

Unusual training gear, advanced computer equipment and at least 10 scientists in white coats lined the gleaming walls. You could park three semi-trailers inside the plane and still have room for a ... Leon!

Zac's older brother was sitting in front of a computer screen. He was busily tapping away at a keyboard, as usual.

'What are you doing here?' asked Zac.

'Oh, hi,' said Leon. 'That Lightning Strike is mighty quick, isn't it. My job is to take you through the equipment for this mission. I'll also help with your training. I think you're going to be very surprised.'

'I'm already surprised,' said Zac. 'A few minutes ago I was off to see the nurse.

Now I find out I'll be in space in three hours!'

The surprises kept coming. Zac saw a small, pink nose poke out of Leon's jacket pocket. Whiskers on the nose twitched and then a whole head popped out for a look around. A rat's head!

'Looks like everyone's along for this mission,' said Zac pointing at the rat. 'Even our pet!'

The rat was Cipher, the smallest member of the Power family.

'I had to bring him along,' said Leon, tickling Cipher under the chin. 'I could tell he was feeling lonely and there was no-one home to ratty-sit him.'

Cipher scampered onto a desk and started munching on a Chocmallow Puff. It was the size of his head! Chocmallow Puffs were Zac's favourite breakfast cereal. It looked like they were Cipher's as well.

'Family reunion is over, boys,' said Agent Shadow impatiently. 'Here's the deal: we know that BIG has a new secret base on the Moon called Lunar Strike. BIG will use the Lunar Strike base to somehow cause chaos on the internet.'

'Sounds like a distraction to me,' said Zac.

'Exactly,' said Agent Shadow. 'What they're really after is money from the

Rockathon. BIG's Agent Mirror is already inside the Space Fortress, organising the robbery.'

Leon continued. 'The Space Fortress is a heavily guarded bank computer that orbits Earth. Seconds after the Rockathon begins, millions of dollars in donations will be sent, via the internet, from all parts of the world. All the donations will pass through the Space Fortress. That's where BIG will steal the money from!'

'We don't have exact details,' added Agent Shadow. 'That's what makes this mission so dangerous. We know next to nothing about this Agent Mirror. Obviously there's not enough time for you to get to the Moon, so your only chance is to get into the Space Fortress.'

Leon looked worried. 'All security is computer-controlled on the Space Fortress. Motion detectors, laser canons, tracking missiles, space torpedos – the works! The whole space station is encased in armour plating one metre thick. We don't know how Agent Mirror got in, but he's already tampered with the master controls!'

'Time is tight, Zac,' added Agent Shadow. 'Three hours training is all we can afford to give you. The Rockathon begins at 7 p.m. tomorrow night – on the other side of the world. With the 12-hour time difference, you MUST complete the mission by 7 a.m. tomorrow – no later!'

'Oh,' said Leon, 'and Mum – I mean Agent Bum Smack – says you have to be home by 8 a.m. to get to guitar practice!'

Zac rolled his eyes. 'Great!'

'Leon will brief you on your equipment while we prepare for take-off,' said Agent Shadow briskly. 'You'll be weightless in space and you need to learn to handle it. We'll be airborne in 25 minutes – get cracking.'

'I've got some fantastic gear for you,' said Leon, leading Zac over to a work bench. Four GIB scientists were waiting to help with the demonstration. 'First up, the Space Master. I tweaked the technology of the Chameleon suit that you used on your last mission. I combined it with a space suit of my own design.'

One of the scientists passed over a folded black garment. Leon took it and shook it out.

'I've set it for plain black colouring at the moment,' explained Leon. 'That'll be the best camouflage for moving around undetected in space. The suit is fully pressurised and heated. Space has no air pressure and is dreadfully cold. Without the suit on you'll explode and then freeze into a lot of VERY messy ice-cubes.'

'Nice work, Leon,' said Zac, slipping into the Space Master. 'Light, comfortable, a good fit. It looks sweet in jet black!'

Leon smiled – he was very proud of himself. 'This belt completes the suit,' he added, as another scientist handed over more equipment. 'The buckle controls suit colour, temperature and pressure – quite simple. There's a specially designed pouch for your SpyPad, along with everything else you'll need.'

Zac wrapped the wide belt around his waist and secured the control buckle. He fitted his SpyPad into its pouch. He flipped the top on one of the other pouches and pulled out a tiny, silver cylinder the size of a small battery.

'Ah,' said Leon, going into full nerd mode. 'Your oxygen supply. I've packed you six of those mini-tanks. They're exactly like the air tanks used for underwater diving.'

'They don't look like they hold much air,' said Zac, lifting the cylinder to his ear and shaking it.

'Careful, Zac!' said Leon. 'The oxygen inside is under extreme pressure. That's how we can keep them so small. That mini-tank fits into your Stealth Master helmet and will give you hours of air. Be warned though, you MUST keep them away from excessive heat at all times.'

'Otherwise?' asked Zac, replacing the delicate, teeny tank in its belt pouch.

'That thing could go off like a grenade!' said Leon, looking very serious.

'What about these?' asked Zac, fiddling with a number of small, metal SpyPad discs he had found in another belt pouch.

'My own invention,' smiled Leon. 'They're a selection of nasty computer viruses that you can spread using your SpyPad. Each one comes with its own instructions. I thought they might come in handy.'

The engines of the Hercules began to rumble. Zac and Leon grabbed the workbench to steady themselves as the monstrous plane taxied down the runway.

Agent Shadow returned from the cockpit. 'Everyone strap themselves in good and tight,' he yelled above the engine noise. 'Everyone except you, Zac. Time for your zero gravity training.'

The Hercules climbed steeply and levelled out at high altitude. Agent Shadow gave a nod to one of the scientists, who then hit a switch. Leon and the crew checked their safety belts. The lights inside the Hercules blinked on and off for a split second.

Zac heard a quiet hum in the walls…

and bumped his head on the roof! He hadn't even noticed the zero gravity generators kick in – he was floating six metres above the metal floor!

'This plane is used for astronaut training,' Agent Shadow explained. 'Best place for you to learn.'

Zac hit his bum a few times over the next five minutes. Luckily all those hours Zac had spent surfing meant that he very quickly got used to being upside-down and off balance.

When he got the hang of zero gravity he began zooming about inside the plane. He even swooped Leon and gave him a good fright.

It was like the best fun-park ride ever – without having to buy a ticket!

Zac was disappointed when he had to stop. The three-hour session just flew past.

'Time's up,' said Agent Shadow. 'There's barely 14 hours to complete this mission. Let's introduce you to your last piece of equipment.'

Chapter 5

'Bring it up,' said Agent Shadow, signalling one of GIB scientists. A metal trapdoor in the belly of the plane slid to one side. A hydraulic platform rose through the floor.

Before Zac was an extraordinary, futuristic spacecraft, painted blazing yellow and red.

'All right!' he said, excited.

Agent Shadow led Zac over to the spacecraft. 'This is the Star Master, GIB's mini-space shuttle. It's the smallest vehicle capable of manned space flight. You'll be taking it out for the first test run, Agent Rock Star.'

Zac leapt into the cockpit of the Star Master. 'I can't wait to get this beauty up to top speed,' said Zac, running one hand down the smooth hull of the spacecraft.

It had the lean looks of a jet fighter and the rocket engine muscle of an advanced NASA shuttle.

Zac immediately began punching some buttons and running pre-flight safety checks. He booted up the navigation computer, checked the star maps and programmed a course to the Space Fortress. After fitting his Stealth Master helmet, he gave the thumbs up.

'Drop the ramp and I'll power up the rockets,' said Zac, keen to get moving. 'Anything else I need to know?'

'Be very careful approaching the Space Fortress,' warned Agent Shadow. 'The station's sensors will detect anything – human or machine – that comes near. If you're not careful, you'll be blasted to space dust!'

'Here,' said Leon, passing over the cereal box. 'Take the Chocmallow Puffs in case you need a snack. Good luck!'

Zac sealed the cockpit of the Star Master. Everyone stood well back. The loading ramp on the Hercules opened slowly and a strong wind rushed inside the plane. Zac pressed the ignition buttons and the rockets thundered.

Zac gripped the joystick and edged the Star Master forward. He hit the mini-shuttle's throttle on the final few metres of the ramp. The spacecraft dropped out into the sky and fired upwards.

The speed was incredible. Soon the Hercules was a speck in the distance. It wouldn't be too long before he reached the outer atmosphere. Zac made himself comfortable and bent down for the box of Chocmallow Puffs. He hadn't eaten anything since lunchtime. The zero gravity training was a tough workout and his stomach was grumbling.

Something inside the cereal box wriggled. Zac let go of the joystick in fright. The Star Master swivelled onto its back and dived towards the ground!

Zac planted his feet firmly on the floor. He yanked on the joystick and wrestled the mini-shuttle back under control. Chocmallow Puffs flew about the cockpit and the box landed on his knees. A furry bundle jumped out into his lap.

'Cipher!' said Zac in surprise.

CHOC
MALLOW
PUFFS
CHOC
MALLOW
PUFFS

At some point during the zero gravity training session the rat must have crawled inside the cereal box, looking for food. Now Zac had an extra passenger.

'This is a dangerous mission!' Zac scolded the rat. 'I can't have stowaways along for the ride.'

Cipher's nose wiggled, his little black eyes blinked.

Zac checked the time. It was 7.09 p.m. He had less than 12 hours to get the job done. He couldn't turn back just to drop off his pet rat!

The sky began to darken. The mini-shuttle was moments from entering space.

'All right, Cipher,' said Zac. 'I hope you

can follow orders. You're about to become the world's first rat-stronaut.'

The Star Master was surrounded by darkness. Zac gazed at the stars. They were astoundingly bright with no air pollution in the way. He banked the mini-shuttle to get one last look at Earth. It was a colossal, glowing ball in blue, green and white. Maybe he could do some space sightseeing on the trip back.

Within a few hours Zac was getting near the Space Fortress.

I really don't feel like dodging laser canons and space torpedoes, Zac thought. *I need to find somewhere close by to leave the shuttle, then I can space-hop over to the Space Fortress in secret.*

Zac checked the computer's star maps for a good place to park. His best bet was an asteroid field nearby.

In another 25 minutes they had reached the asteroid field. The Star Master coasted right into the middle of the swarm of swiftly moving rocks.

'Hey, Cipher,' said Zac, jerking the joystick left and right to avoid colliding with the rocks. 'This is just like my *Pluto Pilot* computer game – but a whole lot better!'

Asteroids came at the mini-shuttle from all directions. There were hundreds of them. Some were the size of a basketball, others were bigger than a house! Zac kept the Star Master ducking and diving through the field of space rocks.

He located an asteroid that looked like it could hide a bulldozer. An excellent parking spot. Zac pulled the mini-shuttle alongside and gently touched down.

Zac looked at the time. It was 11.41 p.m.

Zac carefully scooped up the rat. He pulled out the collar of his Space Master suit and tucked Cipher down the front. Zac loaded his helmet with one of the tiny oxygen tanks and hit the emergency release on the cockpit canopy. He unfastened his seat belt and felt himself drift upwards.

Zac crab-walked across the asteroid. On the other side of the jumbo space rock he made a very interesting discovery. Clamped firmly to the rough surface of the asteroid was a spacecraft. It was painted a girly pink, with flowers all over it. 'Double Trouble' was sprayed along the side.

'Hey, Cipher,' said Zac with a laugh. 'This Agent Mirror tough guy is flying a Barbie rocket!'

Zac moved closer to check out the spacecraft. It was a decent ship, looked fast and had a roomy cockpit. But it was no Star Master.

Zac hid behind a rocky ledge. He peeked carefully over the top into the endless space beyond. In the distance, there it was – the Space Fortress.

It *was* a fortress! Zac could make out the laser canons sweeping back and forth, looking for a target. Dozens of tracking missiles poked from lethal launchers. It bristled with satellite antennae, radar dishes and aerials.

The sensors must be set to pick up human intruders and spacecraft only! thought Zac.

Zac realised the sensors would have to ignore the asteroids, otherwise the automatic security computer would waste all day zapping every speck of space dust that came within range.

All I have to do is hitch a ride on a rock, thought Zac.

Zac tapped the controls of his SpyPad and began scanning some nearby asteroids. He needed something the size of a small car – big enough to stay hidden behind until the last minute. He locked in the perfect asteroid.

Zac sprung from his hiding place. He somersaulted twice and landed like a ninja on his chosen rock.

Cipher did NOT enjoy being in space. He fidgeted about inside Zac's suit, squirmed under his arm and down the sleeve.

'Hey, hold still,' said Zac, gripping the asteroid. 'That tickles!'

The speeding asteroid was drawing close to the Space Fortress. Any second now Zac would have to ditch his ride and leap onto the hull of the huge space station. He relaxed his grip on the rock and curled into a ball. He hoped his rolling motion would fool the security sensors long enough to land on the Space Fortress.

Zac landed with a soft thud. He was out of immediate danger. The security system wouldn't shoot a tracking missile at itself! Scuttling quietly across the Space Fortress, he spotted a maintenance hatch.

Zac flicked the SpyPad selector to Laser and used it as a cutting torch. The Space Fortress was protected by solid steel, but the small hatch was attached to a couple of hinges that melted like cheap chocolate.

The red-hot metal cooled quickly in

the bitter cold of space. Zac tugged the hatch back and slipped inside. He found himself in a tight tunnel used for electrical cables. Taking care not to squish Cipher, Zac crawled forwards until he discovered an airlock into the Space Fortress.

Inside the airlock, Zac took off his Stealth Master helmet. He felt around inside his space suit and grabbed Cipher. Out in the light the rat let out a tiny sneeze and blinked in confusion. Zac dropped him into the helmet for safety.

The Space Fortress was like an immense maze. Passageways lead in every direction. He needed to stay camouflaged. He spun the buckle-dial on his Space Master suit and changed the colour to match the white walls.

Zac came across countless rooms full of complex equipment. He lost valuable time searching for clues to BIG's plan – and Agent Mirror.

Zac moved silently down a long white corridor, looking for the control centre. A murmur at the far end of the corridor caught his attention. Activating the multi-directional microphone on his SpyPad, Zac tuned in to the conversation. He could make out a voice coming through from the distant Lunar Strike base on the Moon.

'We have the Electromagnetic Pulse Beam on standby,' said the voice, crackling across space. 'We will activate on your signal. I need a situation report, Agent Mirror.'

Zac crept closer to the room where the conversation came from, and took a gamble. He poked his SpyPad around the corner of the open door and snapped a quick photo with the built-in camera.

Crouching in the corridor he checked the photo on the screen. What he saw amazed him.

On the SpyPad screen were two girls – identical twin girls!

'Pinky only needs a little more preparation before she can commence hacking into the Space Fortress system,' said one of the girls.

CLICK!

'Superb work,' replied the voice from Lunar Strike. 'Britney, once we scramble the webcast you will have less than five minutes to steal the Rockathon donations. We need that money swiftly transferred from the Space Fortress account to our secret BIG account. Gone without a trace. Understood?'

'You can count on it,' promised Britney.

Zac had never expected this. The mysterious BIG agent was actually a pair of girls? Now was a good time to check in with GIB headquarters. Zac sneaked back the way he'd come.

He ducked into an empty storage locker and dialled Leon's direct number using the

SpyPad's satellite phone.

'Zac, any news?' asked his brother, as soon as he appeared on the screen.

'Big news,' whispered Zac. 'And I mean BIG news. Agent Mirror is actually twin girls, called Pinky and Britney! I don't have much time. I overheard some of their plan. What can you tell me about an Electromagnetic Pulse Beam?'

'EPB, eh? Interesting,' said Leon. 'Latest weapons technology. If they have one, the Lunar Strike base could send out a concentrated electromagnetic burst aimed at Earth. Harmless to humans but totally fries all electronic equipment. A single EPB blast would crash every computer running the Rockathon webcast.'

'Thanks for the tip. I'm going to – '

But Zac never finished the sentence. Two metal claws closed around him, pinning his arms to his side. He struggled to break free.

The more he struggled, the tighter the claws gripped him. Zac could see stars – but they weren't in space!

Zac's feet thrashed about in mid-air. He looked around at his captor, and saw that it was a **HUGE ROBOT.**

The robot towered above him, as tall as a professional basketballer. It was built like a tank but was also painted dazzling pink – the same colour as the Double Trouble rocket.

The robot had arms that belonged on a construction crane. They ended in lethal claws that could obviously crush a car.

The robot was carrying him straight back down to the room he'd been spying on. Struggling to remain upright, he saw the twin girls step into the corridor.

'Intruder located and captured!' said an artificial voice behind his head.

'Drop him!' commanded the one called Britney.

Zac hit the cold floor, face first. It was wonderful to be able to move his arms again.

'Zac Power, I presume?' said the other one, Pinky.

'So this is the spy Lunar Strike warned us might show up,' said Britney, narrowing her beady eyes. 'You don't look like much. Certainly nothing Boltz here can't handle.'

Zac wobbled to his feet and massaged his arms, remembering the claws closing around them.

'So, BIG is still hiring girls?' said Zac, thinking of Caz, the last BIG agent he had encountered.

'Oh, BIG is hiring A LOT of girls,' giggled Britney, winking at her sister. 'Rockets, robots and robbery – that's our business. Right, sis?' She turned to Pinky for a high five.

'At the moment it's robbery,' continued Britney. 'But what say we take a break? We have some time to kill before we can transfer the money. Boltz, bring our guest into the control room. Be gentle – no need for the Gorilla Grip this time.'

Boltz lifted Zac and tucked him under one arm, like you would a bag of chips. It clunked into the control room and tossed Zac into a chair.

'The money transfer will go through in a few hours,' said Pinky. 'Then we'll leave you in peace. Of course, you will be trapped on this space station. But if you behave yourself, we'll play nice and leave you with enough oxygen to breathe.'

'We'll let GIB know where you are,' continued Britney. 'Although when we're finished with you, it might be a bit embarrassing facing a rescue crew. Because, Zac, it's time for – '

'EXTREME MAKE-OVER!' squealed the sisters, clapping their hands.

Pinky fetched a large bag of cosmetics. Britney gave Boltz a nod. The mechanical monstrosity moved in behind the chair and pinned Zac's arms behind him.

'You won't be needing this with what we've got in mind,' said Pinky, snatching Zac's helmet and chucking it into a corner.

She began teasing up Zac's hair with a comb as she whistled an annoying Taylor

Swift tune. Britney got to work with mascara and eye-shadow.

Zac watched precious time tick away on the control room clock. It was already 3.33 p.m. He couldn't believe he was in space, having a make-over at the hands of BIG twin girls!

Pinky was busy spraying Zac's hair with hairspray and using a pencil to colour in his eyebrows.

This is getting ridiculous, Zac thought.

Britney was colouring his cheeks rosy red. On went the dabs of lipstick.

Make these crazy twins stop! thought Zac, wondering how long they could keep this up.

'One more touch,' cackled Pinky, adding so much black pencil around Zac's eyes that he looked like a frightened panda when the girls triumphantly held up a mirror to show Zac.

'C'mon, sis,' said Britney. 'We better head down to the central computer and get ready to scoop the loot!'

Zac looked at the clock again. There were only two and a bit hours left to save the Rockathon. *Will that be enough time?*

The Mirror twins skipped out of the control room, leaving Boltz to watch over Zac.

Zac could hear the metal beast's brain whirring –

Then he heard another sound. He looked down to see Cipher darting between the robot's feet. Boltz saw the rat at the same instant.

No! thought Zac. *I'll be scraping poor Cipher off the floor.*

But Boltz let out a scream that echoed around the control room. Cipher had chewed through the robot's balance cable. It wobbled and then tipped over, crashing to the floor. Flames started shooting from its ears!

'Cipher, my hero!' whooped Zac, leaping to his feet.

But the rat took one look at Zac and scampered back to the safety of the Stealth Master helmet.

'Do I really look that bad?' asked Zac, touching his frizzy hair.

He reached into his backpack and found a tissue, then used it to wipe off the worst of the make-up. He ran a hand through his hair to smooth it down as best he could.

Boltz was out cold, but Zac wasn't taking any chances. He knelt down beside the fallen robot and whipped out his SpyPad. Using the laser he cut through the hatch at the top of its head and unplugged its electronic brain. A final wisp of smoke curled up from the trashed machine and it sagged in a sad heap.

Crunch time. Zac needed to work fast. He dug out the handful of Leon's virus discs and slotted one into his SpyPad. The screen came to life.

CLASSIFIED

– GIB COMPUTER VIRUS –

*Hello, and welcome to the **Mindwarp Worm**. The **Worm** seeks out the source of any unauthorised access and attacks the hacker's own equipment.*

Guaranteed to cause the total collapse of all known computer programs, wipe all hard drives and destroy all files.

Have a nice day, and thank you for choosing this quality Leon Power virus!

*~ **END** ~*

'Sounds nasty,' said Zac, looking over at Cipher. 'If the *Mindwarp Worm* does what it says, we could ruin the Rockathon robbery AND fry all the computers on the Lunar Strike base.'

Zac moved over to the control console and plugged in his SpyPad. He set it to Voice Scrambler. He would still have a sample of Britney talking, from eavesdropping on their conversation. If he could fool the BIG people at Lunar Strike for a few seconds, his plan would work.

Zac cleared his throat and spoke into the SpyPad. 'Testing, testing.'

He surprised himself. The voice that came from the SpyPad speakers was high and whiny – but sounded more like Pinky. It'd do nicely.

He contacted the base. 'Lunar Strike, this is Space Fortress, please respond.'

'This is Lunar Strike. Go ahead, Space Fortress.'

'BIG hacking preparation is complete,' fibbed Zac. 'Request that you network with our central computer for final check.'

'Roger that,' came the reply. 'Network link operational. Lunar Strike out.'

Zac was cutting it close!

He used his SpyPad to inspect the computer files. He discovered that Pinky had already hacked into the system on the Space Fortress and was connected to BIG's secret account. She was all set to steal the Rockathon donations, as easily as taking money out of an ATM.

And that was her mistake!

Zac clicked on the secret BIG account and reversed the transfer. Instead of money going OUT of the Rockathon account, suddenly billions of dollars were being donated to the victims of the tsunami – by a very generous organisation called BIG!

Zac gave a satisfied laugh as he loaded up the *Mindwarp Worm*. He hit send, and Leon's devilish virus went to work.

Within seconds, a panicked voice from Lunar Strike came through the speakers. 'Space Fortress, we have a problem!

TAC
TAC
TAC
TAC
TAC
TAC
00:01
cancelled

Please respond urgently! We are getting severe malfunctions all across the base! Space Fortress, can you provide any information?!'

'This is Space Fortress,' said Zac into the microphone. 'I have some information for you. Eat *Worm*, hackers!'

Suddenly, Zac heard very annoyed shrieks coming down the corridor. The *Mindwarp Worm* had obviously gone to work on Pinky and Britney's equipment as well. They would probably have spotted Zac's 'withdrawal' from BIG's account, too.

Time to bug out, thought Zac, quickly grabbing his helmet and Cipher, and running out of the room.

CHAPTER 10

'Boltz! My beautiful baby Boltz!' wailed Pinky.

Zac glanced back over his shoulder as he raced down the corridor. The Mirror twins were standing in the doorway of the control room staring at the wrecked robot.

'Power, you're finished!' screamed Britney.

Zac broke into a sprint. He dropped Cipher down the front of his Space Master suit as he ran. 'Sorry, little pal,' he said to the rat. 'It's the last time you'll have to travel in my armpit, I promise.'

With his SpyPad set to Locator, Zac scanned the Space Fortress, looking for a likely escape airlock.

'Down here for 20 metres, up two levels, turn right, then straight ahead!'

In a minute, Zac had his helmet back on and was out in space. He looked around for a passing asteroid that would take him back to his mini-shuttle. With some frantic space dog-paddling, and even some galactic back-stroke, he made it!

Zac knew the furious Mirror twins weren't far behind. He jumped into the Star Master and sealed the cockpit. He punched the engine ignition button. He did a sweeping turn around the Space Fortress and pointed the mini-shuttle towards Earth.

The Double Trouble rocket was right on the tail of the Star Master for a few moments until –

KABOOOOOOOOM!

Zac breathed a sigh of relief as he looked in the rear-vision mirror. The twins had crashed the Double Trouble into an asteroid and damaged the engine – a smoking tangle of metal was where the tail fin used to be! In the rocket's cockpit he could just make out Pinky and Britney, red-faced and bellowing, making *very* rude gestures in his direction.

Zac lifted Cipher out of his suit. 'Couldn't have done it without my robo-buster rat!' he said, putting Cipher on the floor.

His SpyPad beeped. 'Zac, Agent Bum Smack here,' said his mum. 'I hope you remember you have a guitar lesson this morning!'

'Sure, Mum,' groaned Zac, trying to sound interested. 'I'm on my way now.'

He hung up the phone.

Zac couldn't believe he was in *space*,

and had just escaped from those maniac Mirror twins, and was still stuck with a boring guitar lesson!

Suddenly Zac had a thought. As he steered the Star Master through the Earth's upper atmosphere, he made a decision. He set a course for the other side of the world ... and the Rockathon!

If he was quick he could catch the end of Axe Grinder's set and still make it to his guitar lesson. Even if he missed his lesson, surely watching Ricky Blazes live in concert would be the greatest guitar lesson he could ever have?

There was a short landing strip right near the massive outdoor stadium. Zac could see the private jets and helicopters of all the stars lined up beside the runway. He touched down and taxied skilfully to the far end.

Zac bolted towards the stadium. He set his Space Master suit colour back to black. It wasn't much of a disguise but it would have to do.

It was sell-out show. Zac wondered how he'd get inside the stadium without a ticket. He was sneaking around the backstage area when he was stopped by a muscle-bound security guard.

'This way, this way! Quickly, Mr Blazes!' said the bouncer, taking Zac by the arm.

Zac was very confused, but didn't argue.

'Here he is!' the guard called out to a worried-looking stage manager.

Now Zac was utterly bewildered.

'Really, Ricky,' said the stage manager, obviously quite annoyed. 'We told you not to move too far from the stage. The rest of the band is waiting to go back on stage to play the encore.' The stage manager passed Zac a guitar, and helped him strap it on.

'There's been a mistake,' Zac tried to explain. 'I'm not who you think – '

But the stage manager wouldn't listen. He pushed Zac up a short flight of stairs that led to the stage. 'Just one encore, *Sonic Boom*,' he whispered. 'The boys are counting on you to do an extra special job. Hey, where did you get that rat? Nice touch! The crowd will go berserk.'

The whole bizarre situation was becoming clear to Zac. Black jumpsuit, cool hair, outrageous eyeliner. He and Ricky Blazes looked like twin brothers!

Suddenly Zac caught a glimpse of the real Ricky Blazes sitting in a dim corner. He was gulping down a cold drink and paying no attention to the madness going on around him.

Before Zac could utter another word the stage manager pushed him on stage. The roar of thousands of people shook the stage as Zac took his place next to the band's singer.

Axe Grinder's lead singer yelled into the microphone. 'This is the first ever live performance of our new single. I hope you're ready to ROCK!'

Listening to *Sonic Boom* 86 times in a row had finally paid off. Zac knew every note by heart. He leapt about the stage, making sure that the billions of people watching the webcast would never forget THIS Axe Grinder show!

When Cipher climbed onto Zac's shoulder, and then hopped onto his head, the huge crowd erupted like a volcano! Hundreds of stage divers and crowd surfers flew in every direction and the applause was deafening.

By the time he was finished, Zac was dripping with sweat and shaking with excitement.

The song seemed to fly by. Next thing Zac knew he was being helped off stage by the road crew. All the members of Axe Grinder were slapping him on the back and congratulating him on his playing. Cipher was still on top of Zac's head.

As they walked back to the change room tent they spotted the real Ricky Blazes wrestling with five security guards.

'Let go of me!' he yelled. 'I told you, I'M RICKY BLAZES!'

'No fans allowed backstage,' said one of the bouncers as they dragged him away.

'Time to go!'

'Fellas, it's been fun,' said Zac, shaking hands with the members of Axe Grinder. He passed the guitar back to the stage manager and pointed towards Ricky Blazes. 'But you should really go and rescue your guitarist.'

The leader singer's jaw dropped.

'Yeah,' said Zac Power with a shrug. 'You see, Cipher and I have a guitar lesson to get to.'